GOLDEN SING ALONG™

KIDS' SONGS WITH CRAZY SOUNDS

A GOLDEN BOOK · NEW YORK
Western Publishing Company, Inc., Racine, Wisconsin 53404

Arrangements by Patrick Kusina and Greg Klas
Characters concepted and illustrated by Michael Strouth

© 1992 Western Publishing Company, Inc. All Rights Reserved.

Published and distributed by Western Publishing Company, Inc. Electronic unit manufactured in China. Printed in U.S.A. No part of this book may be reproduced or copied in any form without written permission from the copyright owner. All trademarks are the property of Western Publishing Company, Inc. ISBN NO. 0-307-74302-0.

This product or its components protected under one or more of the following U.S. patents and other patents pending: 4,209,836; 4,209,844; 4,331,836; 4,304,964; 4,344,148; 5,209,665.

I'VE BEEN WORKING
ON THE RAILROAD

I've been workin' on the railroad,
All the live-long day.
I've been workin' on the railroad,
Just to pass the time away.
Can't you hear the whistle blowing?
Rise up so early in the morn.
Can't you hear the captain shouting,
"Dinah, blow your horn"?

THIS OLD MAN

This old man,
He played one,
He played knick knack on his thumb,
With a knick knack, patty whack,
Give your dog a bone.
This old man came rolling home.

Verse

Two...his shoe
Three...his knee
Four...his door
Five...his hive
Six...these bricks

Seven...this ov'n
Eight... this gate
Nine...this line
Ten...this hen

ARE YOU SLEEPING

Are you sleeping?
Are you sleeping?
Brother John, Brother John.
Morning bells are ringing.
Morning bells are ringing.
Ding Dong Ding! Ding Dong Ding!

OLD KING COLE

Old King Cole was a merry old soul,
And a merry old soul was he.
He called for his pipe,
And he called for his bowl,
And he called for his fiddlers three.

DEPOT

SHE'LL BE COMIN' 'ROUND
THE MOUNTAIN WHEN SHE COMES

She'll be comin' 'round the mountain
when she comes.
She'll be comin' 'round the mountain
when she comes.
She'll be comin' 'round the mountain,
She'll be comin' 'round the mountain,
She'll be comin' 'round the mountain
when she comes.

BAA, BAA, BLACK SHEEP

Baa, baa, black sheep, have you any wool?
Yes sir, yes sir, three bags full.
One for my master, one for my dame,
One for the little boy who lives down the lane.
Baa, baa, black sheep, have you any wool?
Yes sir, yes sir, three bags full.

WOOL
WOOL
WOOL
WOOL

BARBER
SHOP
COMB

HICKORY, DICKORY, DOCK

Hickory, dickory, dock,
The mouse ran up the clock,
The clock struck one,
The mouse ran down,
Hickory, dickory, dock.

12
11
1
10
2
9
3
8
4
7
5
6

MARY HAD A LITTLE LAMB

Mary had a little lamb,
Little lamb, little lamb.
Mary had a little lamb,
Its fleece was white as snow.

Everywhere that Mary went,
Mary went, Mary went,
Everywhere that Mary went,
The lamb was sure to go.